THE PERPEE

PEENCHY BUGS FROM NEW YORK

MW00803415

Jason Rises to Shine for School

by Deborah Baron Hiester

Illustrated by Catrina Evans

Paperback ISBN 978-1-945169-83-0

Published by
Little Blessing Books
An imprint of
Orison Publishers, Inc.
PO Box 188, Grantham, PA 17027
www.OrisonPublishers.com

Illustrations provided by Catrina Evans.

With profound gratitude to

Bob and Jill Baron, my wise, witty and wonderful parents who breathed belief in me;

David, my one true love, my husband, my daily blessing and eternal partner;

and, of course, Jason, my beloved son, my inspiration and my heart.

To Almighty God goes all the glory.

Jason could never get out of bed in the morning for school. He could sleep through anything! No amount of joking, poking or tickling helped. A radio blaring loud tunes didn't move him. Clanking cymbals in his ear barely caused him to so much as twitch. He simply loved to sleep and refused to get up.

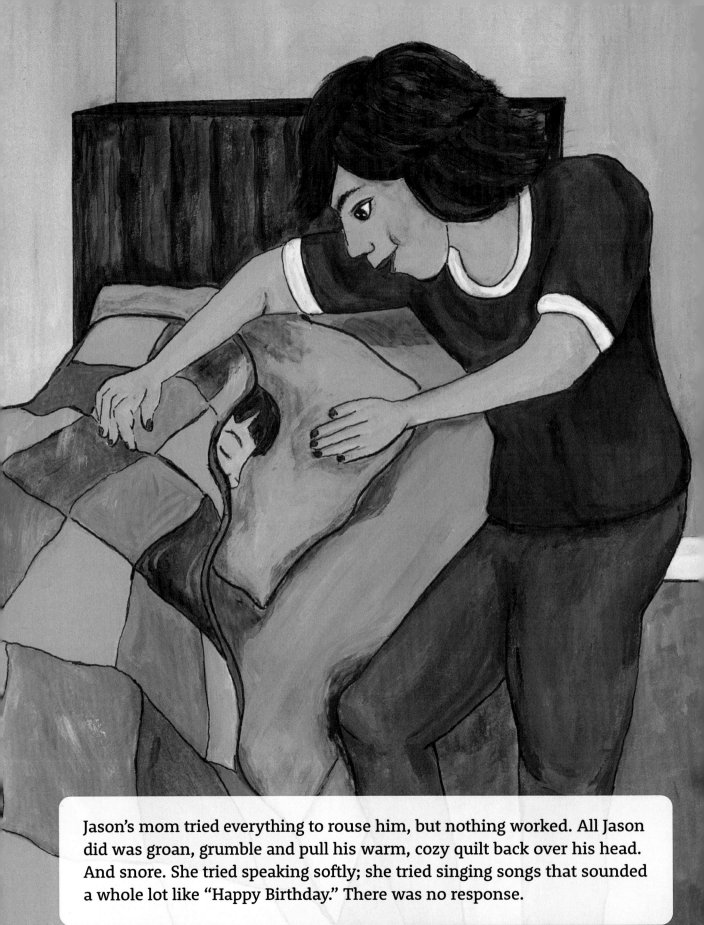

Jason's mom tried everything to rouse him, but nothing worked. All Jason did was groan, grumble and pull his warm, cozy quilt back over his head. And snore. She tried speaking softly; she tried singing songs that sounded a whole lot like "Happy Birthday." There was no response.

But Mom often told him, as she leaned over his bed, "Jason, school is vital to learn and grow." And Jason would *harrumph* loudly, roll his big brown eyes, turn over and go back into his most inviting cuddly dreamland.

As time went on, it got harder and harder for Mom to wake Jason. She even resorted to telling fibs—that school was closed because of a snowstorm (in May) or that it was Saturday (when it was really Wednesday). Surely, Jason would get up now! But he was very smart, and he knew that wasn't the truth. He didn't get up.

As Jason was now officially on Mom's last raw nerve, she was more determined than ever to find a way to get Jason out of bed, for even banging pots and pans together just made him yawn and stick his head underneath his big, fluffy pillow.

Now, what you must know is that Jason was not lazy. He simply chose to invest his energy in things he liked—things that were fun and that he was good at, and he didn't think school was either. That's what he wanted you to believe. Even though it wasn't cool, he secretly loved school. But he loved sleeping even more.

Scratching her head, Mom looked to God for direction. Then she sat still and waited. Her prayers answered, she found the solution in the latest issue of *Cool Mom Magazine*. This move would be extreme; it would be unusual, but Jason's mom was at her wit's end. She would call on experts with a proven track record of success in getting sleepyhead snoozeballs out of bed. There was only one call to make, and that was to The Perpeens, the Peenchy Bugs from New York.

Mom read that The Perpeens would respond only if that call was delivered in a certain manner, using the right words, in the right order, in the right tone, at the right time—and either the entire clan or no one at all would come. They were picky, and there was no rhyme or reason to their decisions. So, Mom could only hope that The Perpeens would answer her call.

Gathering her courage and her shrill loud voice that could send fierce one hundred-pound dogs into hiding, Mom followed the bizarre directions in *Cool Mom Magazine*. She counted slowly and loudly, "1, 2, 3, 4, 5, 6, 7, 8, 9, 10, 11, 12 ... PERPEEN." Then she covered her ears as she blared the ancient call in her "last ditch effort" for help that would arrive quickly.

Mom bellowed even louder. "All Level 4 Watoosis report for duty! All Level 3 Snigglehimers rise and shine! All Level 2 Serene Kumquats elevate and roll! All Level 1 Blackhawk Lalas become vertical! We need your help *now*!"

The dreadful silence that followed was interrupted by the rhythm of loud ... snoring. Mom sighed and continued to wait patiently and quietly, not knowing what would happen next. She was watching Jason sleep, hopeful that her call would be answered. It seemed like hours before she heard the strange cadence of little feet marching totally out of order, coming closer and closer. It was only a matter of moments, though, when Mom heard the rickety old voice of The Perpeens' leader commanding the family to hurry and march in single file to help in this emergency.

"Time's a-wasting! We have a job to do, so move along, everyone!" crackled Crinkum-crankum, Grandfather Perpeen. The clan's lovable patriarch and a unique bug called a "four-legged flong," Crinkum-crankum was highly revered for his life experiences, his incredible vocabulary, his integrity and his razor-sharp wit. Always wearing a dark blue soldier's cap, Crinkum-crankum commanded respect through both his words and his actions.

At last! The Peenchy Bugs arrived at Jason's bedroom door and awaited their invitation to enter his room. After all, they had good manners and were very polite. Jason's mom was thrilled to welcome them. "I'm excited that you're all here! Jason will not get up, and I don't want him to miss even one second of school. It's so important to learn and grow!" she said.

Crinkum-crankum introduced himself to Mom and observed the sleeping boy, who was lying on his stomach with his arms crossed, creating a nest for his head. *Whoosh!* He jumped lightly onto Jason's shoulder and whispered in his ear, "Jason, it's time to get up for school." Dead air. No response. Nothing. Zilch. Nada. A second, louder attempt proved futile. A third was a major waste of time.

Crinkum-crankum was confident he knew who to enlist from his many family members to get this boy out of bed. He thought, *This is a job for a fearless bug who is forceful and kind and can motivate a sleepyhead snoozeball.* Who better to call than identical twins Begbo and Bobji? Begbo and Bobji were bugs called "galloping gimflons." They were lightning fast, feisty, colorful and relentless. Their long, muscular legs stuck out from their multi-colored tunics emblazoned with bright yellow lightning bolts.

They climbed up on Jason's shoulders, one on the left and one on the right. They counted to three and, sticking their tiny wet fingerlings into his ears, buzzed, "Jason—*buzz buzz*—Jason—*buzz buzz*—Jason—*buzz buzz*—Jason, Jason, JASON, J-A-S-O-N!" Nothing but a smile came from the sleeping child. Begbo and Bobji tried their best, over and over again, but their buzzes just didn't work.

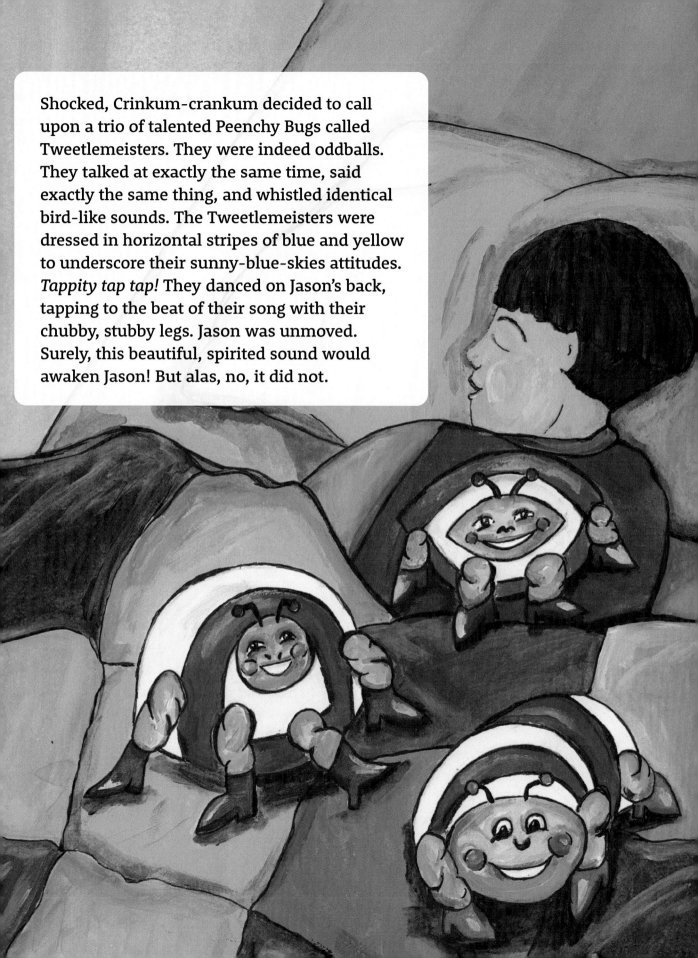

Shocked, Crinkum-crankum decided to call upon a trio of talented Peenchy Bugs called Tweetlemeisters. They were indeed oddballs. They talked at exactly the same time, said exactly the same thing, and whistled identical bird-like sounds. The Tweetlemeisters were dressed in horizontal stripes of blue and yellow to underscore their sunny-blue-skies attitudes. *Tappity tap tap!* They danced on Jason's back, tapping to the beat of their song with their chubby, stubby legs. Jason was unmoved. Surely, this beautiful, spirited sound would awaken Jason! But alas, no, it did not.

Crinkum-crankum was dumbfounded. He needed to bring in a different kind of bug, since none of the others seemed to have any effect at all. He scratched his head and pondered, repeatedly saying with his fingerlings cupping his chin, "Pondering ... pondering ... pondering."

He enlisted *three* high-level squad leaders together, whom he thought would be more powerful, from the Level 4 Watoosis, the Level 3 Snigglehimers, and the Level 2 Serene Kumquats. The head of each musical group was powerful and unusual: Kodie Winklebink had a deep voice that made other Watoosis swoon; August Quincebottom had a British accent for no reason, which baffled other Snigglehimers; and, as with all Serene Kumquats, babbling knobhead Cecil Hannewacker never made any sense to anyone when he spoke.

And so it was that this trio began warming up their tiny voices. "Do, re, mi, fa, sol, la, ti, do!" they sang, over and over and over again, until Mom thought a vein popped in her head. "This is worse than when Jason played the first two lines of Beethoven's *Ode to Joy* every day for a whole year!" Mom shrieked.

Then, just when she couldn't take it anymore, the trio was on the job!
In perfect three-part harmony, they sang the kids' song "Rise and Shine
(Arky, Arky)" (it was the only song they knew) and bounced all over Jason's
back and arms. Jason raised his head, opened his big, brown eyes for a
nanosecond, and … laid his head back down on his folded arms.

"I do declare!" exclaimed Crinkum-crankum. "This is a hard case, indeed! Jason just doesn't want to get up!" He thought deeply for a moment, and then, as though a light bulb lit over his head, wise old Grandfather Perpeen said, "I know now what it will take for Jason to get up, get moving and get to school!" It was to be a part of something bigger than he was—to be a part of a group or a team doing something he loved at school. So Crinkum-crankum called upon his best friend Pimbly Perparpety, the leader of the Level 1 Blackhawk Lalas, and the Lalas leader got right to work.

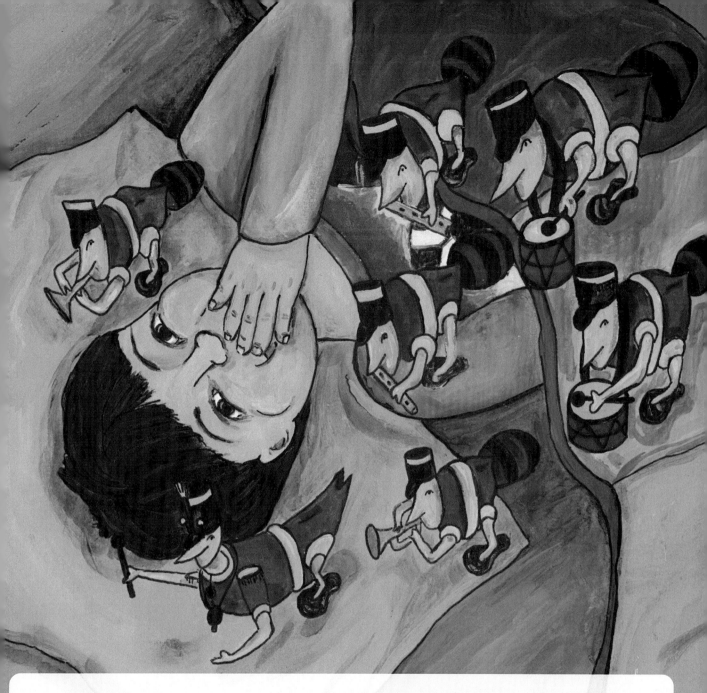

Pimbly was experienced and shrewd. He gave orders to a platoon of Perpeens who were only deployed as a goal-oriented unit. They were known for their odd feet, which looked exactly like small lacrosse sticks. The Blackhawk Lalas, in red and black uniforms, came together—all six mighty warriors. Pimbly blew his black metal whistle, and the troop lined up, ready to move out. This was the extreme corps, the "crème de la crème" of the Peenchy Bugs from New York. With precise marching band-like talent, they performed a drum, fife and bugle song, inviting Jason to join this elite six. *Boomshakalaka!* But he just yawned and declined politely. Pimbly Perparpety was crushed by this most surprising epic failure.

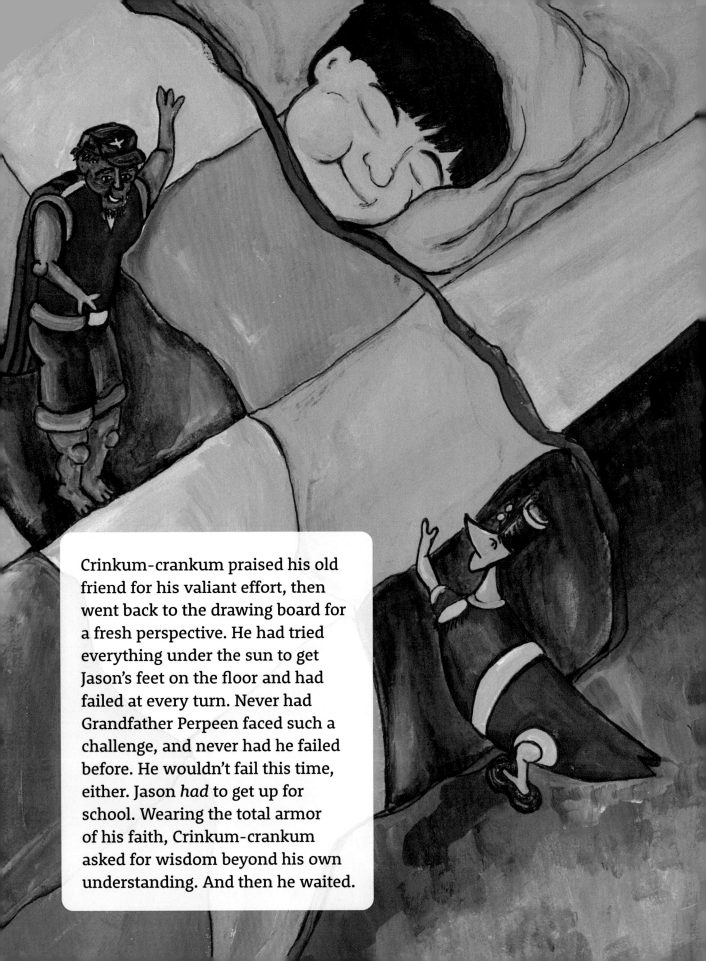

Crinkum-crankum praised his old friend for his valiant effort, then went back to the drawing board for a fresh perspective. He had tried everything under the sun to get Jason's feet on the floor and had failed at every turn. Never had Grandfather Perpeen faced such a challenge, and never had he failed before. He wouldn't fail this time, either. Jason *had* to get up for school. Wearing the total armor of his faith, Crinkum-crankum asked for wisdom beyond his own understanding. And then he waited.

Moments later, his answer was crystal clear. He smiled at the fact that the solution hadn't come to him sooner. In all his attempts, he had employed singing, repetitive noises, whispering, dancing, bouncing on Jason's back and arms, individuals and the special musical forces of the Peenchy Bugs. Except he forgot about one unique Perpeen, one who could relate to Jason in a way no one else could replicate. Crinkum-crankum summoned his own personal favorite Perpeen (although he wasn't supposed to have any): DollBaby. *Everybody* loved DollBaby.

While DollBaby made her way into Jason's room, Crinkum-crankum wrangled several tried-and-true powerhouse Perpeens: Aubrey Schmink, Dudley Poole, Melvin Yarfel and Gertie Schmerl. These bugs just clicked. Literally! To some their music would be annoying; to others it was a joyful noise. These Perpeens clicked with glee in different tones at different speeds. If you closed your eyes (like sleepyhead snoozeballs do), you would think you were deep in the middle of a dense forest at dawn's first light. This quartet gave it their all, but again, Jason did not awaken. So now it was up to DollBaby.

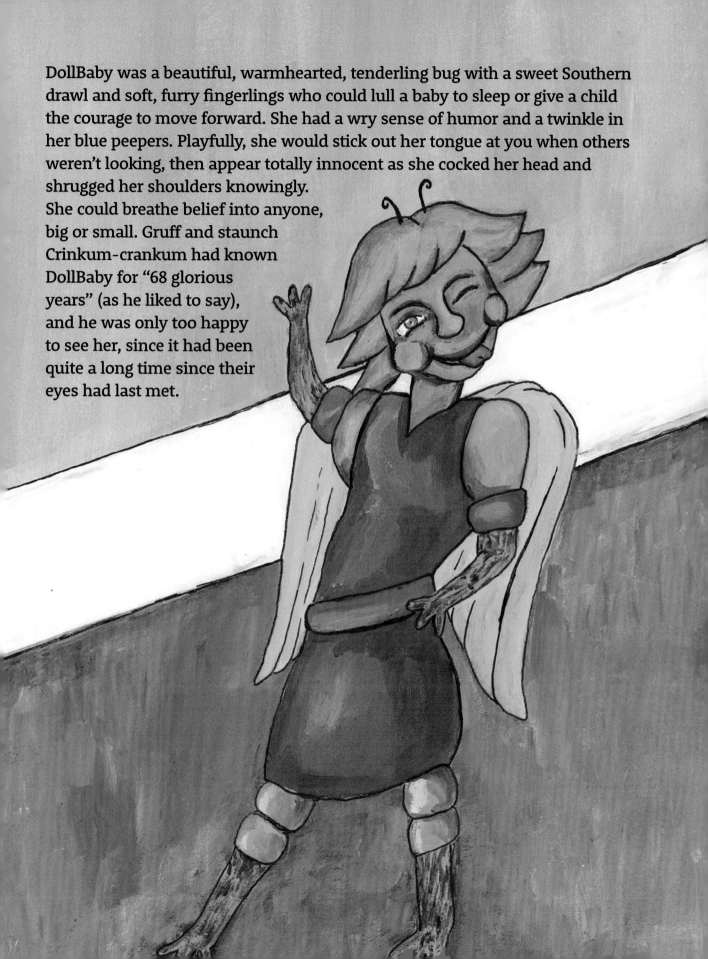

DollBaby was a beautiful, warmhearted, tenderling bug with a sweet Southern drawl and soft, furry fingerlings who could lull a baby to sleep or give a child the courage to move forward. She had a wry sense of humor and a twinkle in her blue peepers. Playfully, she would stick out her tongue at you when others weren't looking, then appear totally innocent as she cocked her head and shrugged her shoulders knowingly.

She could breathe belief into anyone, big or small. Gruff and staunch Crinkum-crankum had known DollBaby for "68 glorious years" (as he liked to say), and he was only too happy to see her, since it had been quite a long time since their eyes had last met.

When DollBaby strolled in, Crinkum-crankum's knobby knees knocked together, and he shrieked with glee, "*Yippee!*" DollBaby matched his excitement with hers, and together they hatched a plan. This one had to work! She would jump on Jason's shoulder and sing to him as she patted his back with her soft, furry fingerlings. And so she did. The other Peenchy Bugs gathered around, held their breath and watched.

Crinkum-crankum marveled at the fast transition in this sleeping boy, who was waking up excited for the day. As DollBaby sang "Your Steller Life: Jason's Song" sweetly to him, he began to set his feet on the floor. Then he propped up his body with his hands on his thighs. As the boy stood up straight, he stretched his hands up high over his head toward the heavens, opened his eyes and said happily and brightly, "Good morning, world!" DollBaby was thrilled that Jason would make this day a wonder-filled one, as she hoped he would make each and every day of his life.

And so it was a good morning, with a great day to follow. Having succeeded in their mission of rousing the sleepy boy, The Perpeens said their fond farewells to Jason and a very happy Mom and left to go back to New York. Crinkum-crankum hugged Mom warmly as she thanked him. Jason was happy to have met them all, and he was excited to see his friends, teachers and especially his teammates at school—to learn and grow through another wonderful day.

Jason knew that each day should be treasured, and he treasured this one for sure! He couldn't wait to tell everyone about his unbelievable morning. Now wanting to rise to shine for school, he was excited by what he could do with his day, whose lives he would touch, and what he would accomplish. Jason realized how precious life is and promised his mom that he would wake up quickly and happily each morning. He remembered what his mom always told him: "Jason," she would say, "it is a blessing to be awake ... and a gift to be alive! Now go and be the best person God intended you to be!"

And so he did.